THE NIGHT BEFORE CHRISTMAS IN TEXAS

Text
Catherine Smith

Illustrations
Steve Egan

Dust Jacket Illustration
Shauna Mooney Kawasaki

SALT LAKE CITY

ISBN 0-87905-485-9
prpk 10: 0-87905-541-3

Published by
Gibbs Smith, Publisher
P.O. Box 667
Layton, Utah 84041

07 06 05 04 14 13 12 11

Printed in China

'Twas the night

before Christmas

in Texas,

you bet,

But no one'd

seen Santa;

he hadn't

come yet.

The chaps were

all hung up,

the boots

neatly shined,

While out

on the plains

a right tough

windstorm

whined.

And Santa

was in it,

with reindeer

and sleigh.

He'd blown in

from Brownsville,

down

Mexico way.

He was squinting

from dust

and his beard

had turned brown.

The reindeer

were squealing;

the sleigh

sinking down,

Till it lurched

to a stop

near the hills

at Big Bend.

Santa said,

"Here we'll wait

for this dust storm

to end.

"The sleigh's

overloaded

with great

Texas toys.

"It's too hard

to steer

in the dust

and the noise!"

Now the problem

was time;

he had Texas

to cross

And the night

passing fast.

Should he get

him a hoss?

But no horse

was nearby;

only longhorns

around.

"I don't trust 'em,"

says Rudolph,

a pawin'

the ground.

So they huddled

to ponder

just what could

be done

To deliver those

toys for

the kids'

Christmas fun.

Things were

downright

disgusting,

when suddenly came

A small Texas

voice calling

Santa

by name...

"Howdy Santa!

Ah'll help!

Ah know just

where tuh go,

"The way tuh

the great

Texas Rangers

ah'll show.

"They kin do it,

ah know,"

chirped the odd

little fellow.

"Well,

by jiminey,"

says Rudolph,

"it's a real

armadillo."

With a leader,

the team quickly

moved north

by east,

Left the

dust storm

in Abilene–

what a relief!

All the Rangers

were called

and they split up

that load,

And giving

a whoop,

all directions

they rode!

San Antonio

children

all sleeping

just so

Heard,

"Y'all have a

good one!

'Member

the Alamo!"

Now

Santa could *fly;*

there was no

time to waste.

On toward Dallas

and Houston

the sleigh sped

with haste.

Heard the band

still performing

at Billy Bob's bar,

And dropped

ten-gallon hats

and new boots

at the door.

He swept into

Dallas,

now feeling

quite jolly,

On Pegasus' neck

placed a

small wreath

of holly.

He rounded

Reunion Tower

heading

toward Irving,

To visit

the Cowboys–

there's none

more deserving!

Dropped

a big load of footballs,

bid the skyline

goodbye.

allas
OWBOYS

"Seasons Greetings,"

he called,

and turned south

on the fly.

All the oil towers

were lighted;

the air seemed

alive

As he headed

toward

Houston

on I-45.

At the

Astrodome,

someone had left

him a treat–

Fresh barbecue,

chili, and

nachos to eat!

45
LONE
STAR
SANTA from ASTROS

"Oh, how I love

Texas!"

Santa sang

with high cheer,

As he passed

Neiman Marcus

drinking Lone Star

"root" beer.

His huge load

of toys got

dropped off,

one by one.

To each

sleeping child

and his dad

and his mum.

Then heading

toward Beaumont,

the whole team

took flight

"Merry Christmas

to Texas!

and to all

a Goodnight!"